DRAGON
GAMES

THE
FROZEN
SEA

DRAGON GAMES

THE FROZEN SEA

BY MADDY MARA

SCHOLASTIC INC.

Copyright © 2023 by Maddy Mara
Illustrations by James Claridades, copyright © 2023 by Scholastic Inc.

All rights reserved. Published by Scholastic Inc., *Publishers since 1920*. SCHOLASTIC and associated logos are trademarks and/or registered trademarks of Scholastic Inc.

The publisher does not have any control over and does not assume any responsibility for author or third-party websites or their content.

No part of this publication may be reproduced, stored in a retrieval system, or transmitted in any form or by any means, electronic, mechanical, photocopying, recording, or otherwise, without written permission of the publisher. For information regarding permission, write to Scholastic Inc., Attention: Permissions Department, 557 Broadway, New York, NY 10012.

This book is a work of fiction. Names, characters, places, and incidents are either the product of the author's imagination or are used fictitiously, and any resemblance to actual persons, living or dead, business establishments, events, or locales is entirely coincidental.

ISBN 978-1-338-85195-3

10 9 8 7 6 5 4 3 2 1   23 24 25 26 27

Printed in the U.S.A.   40

First printing 2023

Book design by Stephanie Yang

IMPERIA

"Luca, Yazmine, and Zane. Come to my desk immediately!"

Luca sat up with a jolt. He had completely zoned out. Had Ms. Long noticed? Probably. She was the kind of teacher who always seemed to know exactly what was going on. But surely Ms. Long would understand why Luca was distracted. After all, how often did you discover the imaginary place your teacher always talked about—Imperia—was not imaginary at all?

He'd found this out when he, Yazmine, and Zane were suddenly transported to Imperia! In Imperia, Luca had turned into a flying, fire-breathing dragon. Zane had become a beast—one that was super big, super strong, and super fluffy. Yazmine had stayed in human form but had the power to become invisible.

At school, the three were not friends. In fact, they barely spoke to one another. But in Imperia, they'd become a team. Their first task had been to battle with a massive lava snake called the Magma Mamba, and safely deliver the Thunder Egg into the Crown of Fire—in a volcano!

They'd been through a lot. It was hard to go back to normal after such a big adventure.

As Luca stood up, he glanced over at Yazmine. She shrugged, a smile twitching at the corners of her mouth. She did not look worried. In fact, her eyes sparkled with excitement. Luca's heart thumped as a new thought crossed his mind. Maybe they weren't in trouble. Maybe they were going back to Imperia!

They had completed the first task. But where there's a *first* task, there's always more! Luca knew there were two other Thunder Eggs to return. That meant two more rounds of this dangerous game they were playing.

Luca, Yazmine, and Zane all arrived at Ms. Long's desk at the same time. It was clear from the grin on Zane's face that he, like Yazmine, was confident they weren't in trouble.

"So, Ms. Long," Zane said, grinning as he ran his fingers through his hair. "Have you got a *task* for us? Is there somewhere *special* you want us to go?"

Zane was either incredibly brave or incredibly foolish to speak to Ms. Long like this. It was sometimes a little hard to tell with Zane.

Ms. Long fixed Zane with a stony stare that made him wilt.

"Yes, Zane," she said. "I do have a job for you three. I need you to go to the gym and clean up the equipment room. The gym teacher tells me that your class left it in a terrible mess."

Ms. Long turned back to the rest of the class.

"What?" Zane protested. "That's not fair! We—"

Yazmine grabbed Zane by the arm and pulled him out of the classroom. Luca followed close behind.

"We dealt with that snake in Imperia," Zane grumbled. "And we beat Dartsmith at his own game. She should be treating us like heroes! But no. We're being punished!"

"Don't you get it?" Yazmine asked, leading

the way down the empty hallways toward the gym. "We're probably going back to Imperia right now. I bet when we open the door to the equipment room, we'll be transported back there!"

Zane went quiet. Luca felt a rush of adrenaline. What Yazmine said made total sense!

The gym was empty when they arrived. The trio made their way over to the equipment room at the back.

"Let me open it!" Zane said. He made a face at the others as he turned the door handle. Slowly, the door pushed back, revealing . . .

A very messy room full of sports equipment.

Luca's heart sank. Zane looked crushed,

too. But Yazmine just shrugged. "No use getting upset about it."

Even so, Luca could tell she was disappointed as well.

In the back corner stood a metal cage where all the balls were kept. There were footballs and soccer balls, volleyballs and basketballs. But the trapdoor at the front of the cage was open and the balls had spilled out all over the floor.

Yazmine waded her way through them and shut the metal trapdoor. "Let's get this job done," she said, pushing up her sleeves and bending low.

They quickly got a good rhythm going.

Luca scooped up a ball and passed it to either Yazmine or Zane. Yazmine dropped the balls in the cage. Zane, being Zane, used it as a chance to practice his basketball skills. He jumped as high as he could to toss the balls into the cage.

As the room started to clear, Luca noticed funny marks on the floor. There was something about the shape they made . . .

"Hey!" he called to the others. "Does this look familiar?"

Zane stared at the squiggly lines on the floor. "It's just like the map that was on the blackboard before we went to Imperia last time."

"You're right! There's Wisdom Mountain,"

Yazmine said, pointing to a toothlike shape in the middle. "And there's the inn and the Crown of Fire. All the places we went to! But hang on . . . what's this?"

Yazmine kicked aside a basketball near the top of the map. Luca squinted at it. *Was it a house? A palace?* It was surrounded by dots that looked a bit like snowflakes. Or insects?

Luca shivered. Maybe they were Dartsmith's army of insect drones. They had been hard to battle last time.

Luca bent down to pick up another ball. The moment he touched it, he knew it was special. It was oddly shaped, and its surface was rough.

"Guys," he said, holding it up. "I think I've found a Thunder Egg!"

"Can I look?" asked Zane. He took it from Luca and inspected it. "It's not the same as the last one. This one's smaller and lighter in color. Maybe it's a different type of dragon? And it's cold."

"I'm not surprised it's cold," Yazmine said. "It's covered in snow."

Luca and Zane stared at her. "What are you talking about? There's no snow on it. How could there be? It's the middle of summer!"

"You can't see it? How very interesting." She stretched out her hands. "Zane, pass it to me?"

Zane did as she asked. The moment Yazmine's hands touched the egg, the sports equipment room—and everything in it—vanished.

The ground fell away and Luca began tumbling head over heels. The air swirling around him grew colder and colder. But the strange thing was, the longer Luca plummeted through darkness, the less the cold bothered him. Perhaps he was getting used to it. Or maybe dragons didn't feel the cold?

Luca squeezed his eyes shut, bracing himself for a hard landing like last time.

But instead of a thud, Luca landed softly. He opened his eyes but immediately closed them again. The darkness had been replaced by blinding brightness. He needed sunglasses!

He heard Zane's voice. "Luca? Is that you?"

Luca opened his eyes just a crack, letting them adjust to the glare. There stood Zane. But he hadn't turned into a beast like last time. In fact, Zane looked exactly like he did in class. The only difference was his clothes. He was wearing leather pants and heavy boots. Slung over his broad shoulders was a thick jacket made of fur. Across his chest was the strap of a bag.

"Of course it's me," said Luca. His voice sounded strange. Kind of growly. "I wonder why you're not a beast?"

Zane smoothed his hair. "Looks like our roles are a different in this round. Hey, I wonder what my special power is?"

Luca wasn't listening. That's because a golden dragon loomed behind Zane. Its whole body glittered in the sunlight. When it breathed, sparkling droplets of ice formed in the air.

Luca stared in awe. Even though he had been a dragon before, he'd never actually met a *real* one. Had this dragon hatched from the Thunder Egg they'd returned on their last quest?

The dragon fixed its gaze on Luca. There was something familiar about its eyes.

"Yazmine?" Luca gasped. "You're a dragon, too?"

A million thoughts leapt into Luca's head all at once. The first one was that he was kind of annoyed. It was cool being the only dragon last time! He'd been the biggest of the group, and the only one who could fly.

But then Luca started to see the upside of Yazmine also being a dragon. It would be fun to have another dragon to fly with. And they could take turns carrying Zane on their backs.

The golden dragon looked down at itself. "Wow! I guess so."

It was definitely Yazmine's voice. Just louder and more fiery! She stretched out her wings and roared. Golden flames billowed from her jaws. She was a very impressive dragon!

"How weird," the Yazmine dragon said. "I thought we'd always take on the same forms in Imperia. But this time, Zane is the human, I am the dragon, and Luca, you're—"

Luca cut her off. "Wait, I'm not a dragon?"

Even as he said it, he half knew the answer. He felt strong, but in a completely different way from his dragon strength. And when he tried to flap his wings, there was nothing to flap. Slowly, he looked down. Last time he had been covered by shining scales. This time he was covered in thick white fur.

"I'm a beast, aren't I?" he growled.

"You sure are!" Zane grinned. "A very nice one, too. And when I say *nice*, I mean repulsive."

Yazmine snorted two perfect, golden smoke rings from her nostrils. "Don't listen to him, Luca. You're a perfect beast. I wouldn't say repulsive. I think ugly is more like it. And hey, at least you're not fluffy! That shaggy white fur of yours will blend in perfectly here. Have you checked this place out?"

For the first time, Luca took a good look around. There was snow as far as the eye could see. To their right were woods, the dense trees capped with snow like a scene from a winter fairy tale. To the left were majestic mountains, also covered in snow and glinting in the sun.

"Better than the stinky equipment room, hey, Zane?" Yazmine laughed, a small flame leaping from her mouth. "Zane?"

They both turned in circles. How strange! Zane had been right there. Now he was gone.

"Maybe his power is invisibility, like yours was?" Luca suggested.

There was a sudden whir of color. Was blurry vision a beast thing? The whirring thing stopped. Luca blinked.

Standing there was a snowman. Zane was beside it, looking pleased with himself. "Not a bad self-portrait, is it?"

Yazmine's huge dragon eyes grew even wider. "You built that fast. Hang on—is your special power hyperspeed?"

Zane grinned. "Yup, you got it in one. Much cooler than invisibility."

"No way!" Yazmine said, but there was a smile on her dragon-y face.

Something about the surroundings seemed familiar to Luca, and he finally realized why. "Ms. Long talked about this area just this week."

Luca had always loved listening to Ms. Long's stories about Imperia. But since learning that Imperia was a real place, Luca had been listening even more carefully. Her stories probably contained useful hints for future visits.

Yazmine nodded. "North Gelida, right? It's

one of the most dangerous areas of Imperia. How did Ms. Long put it? *There's a lot of competition for food, so the creatures here are always on the hunt."*

Luca gulped. It was hard to imagine anything more dangerous than the Magma Mamba, but maybe that monster would end up seeming like a cute pet.

An even more worrying thought hit him. "The Thunder Egg!"

"Relax." Zane tapped the bag slung over his shoulder. "I stowed it in here."

Yazmine's eyes narrowed. "How about I look after it? Or Luca?"

Zane shook his head. "I am the only one

with any real ball skills. This thing's going to be safest with me, believe me."

"It's not a ball, Zane," Yazmine said in her deep dragon voice. "It's an egg. And inside is one of the three future dragon rulers of Imperia."

"I haven't forgotten the prophecy," Zane said. "But I also haven't forgotten that this is a game. We're in a competition with that Dartsmith guy, remember? And when it comes to games, I'm your go-to guy."

"That depends on the game," Yazmine retorted. "There are games that Luca and I are better at."

Zane folded his arms. "Yeah? Like what?"

Before Yazmine could respond, a high, sharp sound pierced the air.

Luca clapped his paws over his ears. "Ouch! What is that whistle?"

"I can't hear a whistle," Yazmine said, "but I can hear a rumbling."

The whistle stopped as suddenly as it had begun. Now Luca could hear rumbling, too.

They all turned to the mountain range, where a mass of snow tumbled toward them at an alarming speed.

"Avalanche!" Luca cried, his heart pounding.

Zane shook his head. His confident smile had faded. "That's no avalanche. That's something much, much worse."

A sinister howling echoed around them.

Luca's beast ears twitched with the sound. "What is that, Zane?"

Zane had a good memory for the many monsters and beasts in Ms. Long's Imperia stories.

"It's an Avalanche Wolf," Zane said grimly. "The main predator in North Gelida. And it's heading this way."

Luca stared at the huge bank of snow plummeting down the mountain. His beast eyes were very sharp. As he watched the avalanche, he saw multiple wolf heads rise up, then disappear back into the snow. *Hang on, did that mean more than one beast was coming?*

Then he realized: All those heads were attached to a single, massive wolf body! That was way worse!

As the monstrous thing galloped closer, the heads stretched up above the snow, baying ferociously. Great clouds of ice billowed in all directions.

Luca watched in horror as trees and boulders were crushed beneath the beast. The terrifying calls grew ever louder.

Fear shot through Luca. "Yazmine, you'd better try flying. It'll take a bit of time to work it out. Don't feel bad if—"

Yazmine gave her wings a flap and rose smoothly into the air. "Thanks, I think I've got it! I picked up some tips from watching you last time. Hey, this is fun!"

"You forgot Zane!" Luca called as Yazmine flew higher.

Bloodthirsty wolf howls ricocheted off the mountains.

As the avalanche thundered closer, Luca saw the enormous beast was like a writhing bank of snow but with countless legs and snarling heads. Luca had read about Cerberus, a mythical dog with three heads. But a massive

snow-wolf avalanche
thingy, with more than
ten heads? It was the
stuff of nightmares.

Now Luca could see
its creepy, pale eyes.
Its many fangs, pointy as icicles, gleamed in
the sunlight.

Yazmine wheeled in the air overhead.
"Sorry, Zane!" she called. "I'll fly back to you!"

"No need," Zane called over the noise. "Just
swoop down over there. I'll catch up with you."

Zane streaked across the ice to meet
Yazmine. She flew lower as he leapt into the
air. A moment later, Zane was safely sitting
on Yazmine's broad dragon back.

"This is the best special power ever!" whooped Zane. "If I could move like this on the football field, I'd be unstoppable."

"Nice work," Luca cheered.

"Luca, watch out!" Yazmine cried.

Luca swung around. The Avalanche Wolf was much closer than he'd realized! It was tearing toward him in a blizzard of snow, its giant paws pounding hard. The monster was constantly shifting and changing. One moment the thing had ten heads, the next it had fifteen.

But it didn't matter how many heads the monster had. The real issue was that all of them were snarling at Luca! Drool fell like ropes from the many enormous jaws as the beast drew closer by the second. Dread churned in Luca's stomach. He felt like a huge wave with teeth was about to crash over him.

Luca heard the others bellowing at him. "RUN!"

Luca did not hesitate. He turned and ran. He hadn't run in his new beast body yet—he really hoped he was fast! Luckily, he was well-equipped for the snowy terrain. His wide, flat feet didn't sink into the thick snow. He half glided across the surface. Running as a beast was almost like skiing!

All the same, Luca could feel the Avalanche Wolf closing in on him. The sound of its slob-bering breath and thundering paws grew louder. Its angry barking filled his ears. Squinting through the brightness, Luca saw a shape up ahead. It was some kind of hut. His heart leapt. If he could just make it that far, maybe he'd be safe!

He turned to check where the wolf was. It had arrived at Zane's snowman. Luca's stomach lurched as the snowy, snarling beast flattened it without slowing.

All that was left was a single broken twig arm sticking straight up.

The wolf surged after him. Through the frenzied barking, Luca thought he heard something else. Words. *Hungry! So hungry!*

Luca gritted his teeth. *Stay focused*, he

urged himself. *Don't start thinking the monster is talking to you!* Luca half ran and half skated on his broad beast feet.

The last time Luca was in Imperia, he had been with Yazmine a lot of the time. They'd figured out things together. But with Yazmine and Zane in the air, Luca felt entirely alone. He had to get through this by himself.

As he neared the hut, Luca saw that it was made of stone. It was clearly abandoned, but it looked sturdy. Phew! Luca looked up to see Zane riding on Yazmine's back. He was leaning over the side.

"The multi-headed snow mutt is almost on you!" Zane yelled.

"I am aware of that, Zane!" Luca growled back.

He concentrated on the wooden door of the hut. It was only a few feet away. Would it be unlocked? It had to be!

When he arrived at the door, Luca didn't slow. He leapt at it, kicking with his huge feet. The door opened easily and Luca crashed through, tumbling onto the floor. Scrambling up, Luca closed the door and leaned heavily against it. He took one gulp of air, and then another.

But it was hard to catch his breath when the Avalanche Wolf roared louder than ever. The stone walls of the hut trembled. Luca had a bad feeling. He pictured the wolf leaping onto the hut, crushing it with its massive body and ripping it apart with its many heads and vicious fangs.

This hut wasn't going to protect him at all. He'd be like the last cracker in a box. Luca's beast instincts kicked in. *Get out. Get out now!*

At the back of the hut was a single window. Without pausing to think, Luca ran at it and dove through. Shards of glass flew everywhere but didn't pierce Luca's tough hide. He landed in the snowdrift behind the hut, then got to his paws as quickly as he could.

Luca turned just as the massive Avalanche Wolf smashed into the hut. Luca knew he should probably run. He needed to get some distance between himself and this monster.

But he stood there, watching as the beast tore the hut apart, the many heads biting through the stones like they were marshmallows. He heard that word again. *Hungry.*

In a flurry of snow, the hut was soon nothing more than a pile of dust.

A new sound rent the air. It wasn't the howling of a wolf or the rumbling of an avalanche.

It was the roar of a furious dragon. Yazmine flew toward the beast from above, her talons outstretched, fire erupting from her jaws.

The many heads of the beast stopped. All those icy eyes fixed on Yazmine as she swooped in, Zane holding on tight. Her talons gouged deep lines into the massive back of the monster. It snarled in fury, its jaws gnashing at Yazmine and Zane.

But Yazmine whooshed away easily. In the air, she turned, wheeling around for another pass. This time, Zane leaned dangerously over the side, swinging his bag like a weapon. The bag with the Thunder Egg inside! As Yazmine flew low, Zane used it to whack a few wolf heads.

Luca winced. It was brave, but also incredibly stupid. What if the egg broke? What if Zane fell off?

The monster leapt up at Yazmine again, but she was ready. She opened her jaws wide, filling the air with flames. They were so bright that for a moment, the surrounding snow turned gold before melting. The acrid smell of scorched fur filled the air. To Luca's amazement, the massive beast turned and thundered away. As it ran off, howling, it shrank in size, slowly returning to the snow.

Within seconds, there was nothing there at all.

With a whoosh of air, Yazmine flew down and landed beside Luca.

"Are you okay?" Zane asked, leaping from Yazmine's back and zooming over to Luca.

Luca blinked. This superfast version of Zane was taking some getting used to.

"I'm fine," Luca muttered. "Yazmine, thanks for fighting that thing off. I . . . don't know what would've happened if you hadn't helped out."

"It's no problem," Yazmine said. "We're a team. That's what we do."

It was true they were a team. But that was the problem: Luca felt like he'd let the side down.

"Hey, look!" Yazmine said, pulling Luca out of his thoughts. "What's going on with the Thunder Egg?"

Zane's bag was glowing. He opened it up and yanked out the egg.

"How about being careful?" Yazmine suggested. "That rock is kind of valuable. Like, the *entire future of Imperia* valuable."

"Stop stressing, Yazmine," Zane told her. "I'm totally responsible."

"Look! The scoreboard is back," Luca said, cutting the argument off before it went any further.

Numbers were glowing on the egg.

2:0

"We only get two points for escaping that bloodthirsty brute?" Zane looked disappointed.

"At least we're up on Dartsmith," Yazmine pointed out. "But it's still anyone's game. Has the map appeared on the other side, like last time?"

Zane turned over the egg. It was blank. But as they watched, a squiggly line began to appear. Like before, it was as if a map was being etched into the rock's surface by an invisible tool. Soon, the familiar shape of

Imperia could be seen, identical to the one on the floor of the sports equipment room.

Up in the northern part was a snowflake. Beside it were three brightly colored dots.

Luca pointed. "That's us."

In the center of the map was another icon, glowing brightly. It was shaped like a tooth.

Yazmine tapped it with one of her gleaming talons. "Wisdom Mountain!" she said. "Looks like we're supposed to go there again."

Luca looked at it doubtfully. Wisdom Mountain was a long way from where they were. Even with his beast strength, would he be able to run all that way? And if he could, how long would it take?

Maybe it was a coincidence. Or maybe the egg sensed Luca's worry somehow. But just then another line began to appear. It snaked out from the snowflake icon to right near Wisdom Mountain.

"It looks like some kind of pathway," Yazmine said, noticing it, too.

"Could be a shortcut," Zane said. He zipped over to Yazmine and was on her back in less than a second.

"Hey!" Yazmine snapped. "How about a little warning before you jump on me?"

"Sorry," said Zane, not looking sorry at all. "C'mon. Let's check out the lay of the land from above. We'll see if we can spot what that squiggly line is. Luca, you run along below."

They headed across the frozen landscape. Luca kept one eye out for what the line might be, and another eye out for predators. The Avalanche Wolf could be back at any moment. And who knew what else might be out here, waiting to attack!

Even with the risks, Luca had to admit that he was having fun. He was getting used to his beast body and loved gliding across the snow at an incredible speed. The wind whipped around him but his thick white fur kept him warm.

A shout came from above. "Luca! We can see something!"

Zane waved his arm wildly, a huge grin on

his face. The bag holding the Thunder Egg swung dangerously back and forth.

The egg will be fine with Zane, Luca told himself. Maybe if he said it enough, it would be true!

"Look up ahead!" Zane pointed.

Through the bright glare of the snowy wilderness, a twisting pathway came into view. It looked like some sort of slide, winding its way through the snow, looping back and forth like a serpent. Curious, Luca ran toward it.

Up close, the strange pathway looked like something out of the Winter Olympics. What was that sport where athletes zoomed along, lying on a flat sled-type thing? The word

popped into his head. *Luge.* Was this the squiggly line they'd seen on the egg? Could it really stretch all the way to Wisdom Mountain? The last time they had been in Imperia, there was no snow around Wisdom Mountain. What would happen to the track once the snow ran out?

Luca heard Yazmine's loud dragon voice. "The line on the map is flashing," she reported. "You're definitely supposed to get on that slide. We'll see you at the Dragon Cave. Good luck!"

With a powerful flap of her shimmering wings, Yazmine took off with Zane on board. Once again, Luca was alone.

The wind howled louder than ever. Or was that the Avalanche Wolf returning? Luca did not intend to find out. He leapt over the raised side of the track. With one push of his powerful beast arms, Luca was away!

Luge looked easy in the Olympics. But Luca soon discovered that it was not easy at all.

Luca had never traveled so fast in his life! His fur flattened out as he hurtled along. The freezing air pushed past him so fast it was hard to breathe. The track was carved directly into the ice. This made it even more slippery! Luca's eyes began to water, but he couldn't lift his arms to wipe them.

Because Luca was lying on his back, he had no idea what bends and twists were coming up. Worse, even the slightest movement of his head or shoulders made him slide up the curved sides of the track.

Luca quickly learned to stay as rigid as possible. He did not want to slip off this thing. Who knew where he would end up!

The ride was intense—and awesome! Once he got used to the incredible speed, Luca felt like he could relax a little. He opened his eyes and gazed at Imperia's sky stretching out above him. To think, that morning he had woken up an ordinary kid in an ordinary bed. Now he was a powerful, shaggy beast, zooming along on an ice track through Imperia!

It was not a typical Thursday, that was for sure.

Then Luca spotted something worrying. A small dark shape had appeared above him. Luca frowned. He could hear a high-pitched whining noise. The shape flew closer.

Now Luca knew what it was: one of Dartsmith's insect drones!

The last time they were in Imperia, Dartsmith had used his drones to spy on them. Clearly, he was doing the same thing again.

I have to destroy it, thought Luca.

But that was going to be very hard. The slightest wrong movement could make him slide off the track. The insect drone hovered closer and closer until it was buzzing directly over his face. Luca saw its bulging bug eyes blink as it took photos of him.

If that wasn't annoying enough, the thing poked Luca with its needlelike nose. *Ouch!* Luca could feel the sharp sting even through his thick hide. *Don't flinch!* Luca told himself. *Keep a steady path.*

The bug whirred over to Luca's other side and stung him there. Back and forth the irritating insect went.

"You're going to lose this round, Dartsmith!" Luca yelled at the drone. If it was taking photos, then it was probably recording audio, too. "Just like you did last time."

Finally, Luca snapped. When the drone was directly above him, Luca clapped his hefty front paws together like he was swatting a fly. The machine crumbled to pieces. Luca slipped up the side of the luge but

managed to correct his path. He grinned. As a normal kid, his reflexes weren't anything special. But the beast version of Luca was lightning fast!

Luca couldn't check the Thunder Egg now, but he was pretty sure destroying that drone would earn them a point.

With the drone destroyed, Luca could again concentrate on his journey. He was not traveling as fast now. The trees that whooshed by on either side of the track had changed, and Luca sensed he was drawing close to Wisdom Mountain. Yet the air was as cold as ever. Confused, Luca lifted his head just enough to peek over the rim of the track. He was in a forest now, but the snow was still thick on the ground. Maybe this was normal. Maybe winter had fallen. But in his heart, Luca sensed that something was wrong.

The track widened and flattened out. Then, without warning, the track abruptly ended, flinging Luca onto a thick drift of snow. It made for a soft landing . . . until it roared and stood up! Luca was thrown onto his back but leapt to his paws quickly.

Before him stood a beast. It looked a bit like a bear, but it was much, MUCH bigger than any bear Luca had ever heard about. Instead of a pelt of fur, the beast was entirely covered in orange, curling leaves, making it look scraggly and unwell. The huge leaf-bear began to growl.

Slowly and carefully, Luca backed away. The bear looked hungry. Hungry enough to rip him apart for dinner.

"Easy now," Luca muttered. "I'm not trying to hurt you."

The bear's growls grew louder. To Luca's

shock, they also grew clearer. He thought of the Avalanche Wolf. He'd thought he'd imagined hearing it speak. But maybe he hadn't. Maybe he could understand beasts now.

"Outsider! Dartsmith warned us three enemies would come. He told us to show no mercy. You want to destroy Imperia!"

The hulking beast lurched toward Luca, its claws and teeth bared. Luca jumped away as the leaf-bear struck out at him.

Fear pumped through Luca's veins. But so did anger. "My friends and I are not trying to destroy Imperia. It's the opposite! We're here to help Imperia find peace again."

Friends. It was the first time Luca had used

that word to describe Yazmine and Zane. But it felt true. At least, it mostly did.

The leaf-bear fixed its amber-colored eyes on him.

"Why should I believe you, snow beast?" it muttered, rustling its crunchy leaves menacingly. The more it spoke, the clearer it sounded to Luca. "It's because of you that the Avalanche Wolf is roaming more and more of Imperia, bringing winter with it."

Luca stared at the bear. "Wait, are you saying that all this ice and snow is because of the Avalanche Wolf?"

"Of course," growled the bear. "It was fine when it stayed in North Gelida. But now it is rampaging everywhere, searching for you and the other Outsiders. It is hungry, too. Dartsmith stopped feeding it, so it will be vicious on the hunt."

Luca felt a chill, remembering how he'd heard the Avalanche Wolf talk about its hunger.

"If someone doesn't stop the wolf, we forest creatures may not survive. Look at my leaves! If I lose them all, I'll have no protection against the cold."

Dead-looking leaves fell from the bear every time it moved.

Luca clenched his jaw. Sure, this leaf-bear was huge and frankly terrifying. But it didn't deserve to suffer because of Dartsmith's cruel ways.

Luca risked taking a step forward. "Dartsmith is a power-hungry fiend," he said. "He will do anything to keep control of Imperia. He knows the only thing that can stop him is the return of the three Thunder Eggs. The future dragon leaders."

The bear's eyes widened. "The prophecy!" it growled softly. "I remember hearing of it, long ago."

Luca nodded. So many lives depended on Luca and the others returning the Thunder Eggs. Dartsmith might think of it as just a game, but their quest was all-important.

"I am on my way to the Dragon Cave. My friends and I need to find out what to do next. Will you help me?"

The bear closed its eyes, lifted its nose into the air, and breathed deeply. Its leaves rustled gently. The bear opened its eyes once more.

"Yes, because I trust you. You have the scent of goodness about you. And I have long suspected Dartsmith is lying. When he came to power, he told the beasts of Imperia that everything would be better for us. He said all our hardships were the fault of the dragons. So we helped him destroy them all." The bear hung its head. "I will never forgive myself for that. Life is far worse now than it ever was when dragons ruled."

The leaf-bear raised a meaty paw, its claws extended. "That path leads straight up the mountain to the cave. Good luck, snow beast.

If you need any bear backup, we will be there."

"Thanks," Luca said. He couldn't quite believe he had managed to talk this bear around. It was lucky that he somehow knew how to communicate with it. After the Avalanche Wolf, Luca had felt like a total failure as a beast. But maybe he had more skills than he realized.

With a final nod at the leaf-bear, Luca sprinted up the mountain path.

In his human form, Luca was not the greatest runner. He especially disliked running long distances. But in beast form, it was easy. Even uphill! Luca pounded up the mountain, pushing aside branches and kicking away rocks that blocked his path.

He was excited to return to the Dragon Cave. It was no ordinary place. It had such a cool atmosphere—powerful, ancient, and just the right amount of terrifying. Standing inside it last time, Luca had been able to communicate with the long-dead dragons of Imperia. It was amazing to connect with this land's history.

The last section of the path was very steep. Luca had to climb instead of run, grasping on to snow-covered rocks and hefting his huge body up. His muscly beast arms made short work of it. As he pulled himself onto the smooth platform outside the Dragon Cave, he heard slow hand-clapping.

"You finally made it!"

Luca looked up. There was Zane, grinning. "Just kidding." He reached out a hand and helped Luca to his feet. "You're actually pretty fast as a beast. Not as fast as hyperspeedy me, but not bad. Also, looks like you earned us more points?"

4:0

"That'll be the drone I was chatting with earlier," Luca said dryly. "And maybe also the bear. Hey, speaking of chatting, turns out I can understand some beast languages when I am in beast form."

"Yeah, I could do that," said Zane.

Luca stared at Zane. "You could understand the animals the last time we were in Imperia? Why didn't you say?"

Zane shrugged. "Didn't seem important. I didn't hear anything useful, that's for sure. It was mostly 'Can I eat that thing?' or 'Is that thing going to eat me?' Got kinda annoying after a while, so I blocked it out."

"Hey, where's Yazmine?" Luca asked, looking around.

"She's gone in already," Zane said, nodding at the cave. "Said the ancient dragons were calling her."

"Yazmine could hear them?" Luca asked.

Actually, that made sense. Yazmine was in dragon form, so of course she'd be able to hear the Ancient Ones. Luca loved hearing their voices last time. Maybe he'd still be able to, even though he was in beast form?

Luca strained his ears. Nope. He felt a tug of disappointment. But then he shook it off.

This time he could understand the beasts of Imperia. Zane might not think it was important, but he did!

He turned to Zane. "Got the Thunder Egg?"

Zane rolled his eyes and pulled it out of his bag. "What is it with you two, always bugging me about the egg? You forget I'm a football star. Keeping your eye on the ball is, like, the most important part of the game. Come on, let's go in."

Luca padded into the cave with Zane. Through the gloom, Luca could make out the intricate drawings of dragons on the cave's walls. Like last time, the eyes of the dragons seemed to be watching them. But this time, Luca's sensitive beast nose picked up strange aromas. Long-ago fires. Sweet-smelling plants that had been burned many moons ago. He could smell that animals had slept in here. Luca frowned. There was another smell. A human had been in the cave recently.

Yazmine stood in the circle of stones, her eyes wide with excitement. "Quick! Get over here. I'm dying to know what the ancient dragons have to tell us."

Zane pulled the Thunder Egg out of the bag as he and Luca stepped into the circle. Once all three of them were inside the ring, the egg began to glow. Soon it lit up the cave, and the drawings on the walls began to move and change. The lines that had been dragons re-formed into a jet shape.

Luca's stomach clenched. Dartsmith!

More lines appeared. Some made snowflake shapes. But as Luca watched, the snowflake drawings drifted down to where the wall of the cave met the floor. Slowly, something began to rise up out of the snow pile. Shark-fin shapes emerged, like tall waves. Then in the middle of these came another strange shape. Luca squinted. *Was that a house?* No, too grand. *A palace?* Other lines appeared around it, like waves on the ocean.

Now Luca was really confused. "Yazmine, what are the Ancient Ones saying?"

Yazmine raised a talon, her head tilted. "They are happy we won the first round," she reported, smiling. But her smile began to fade

as the rumbling voices continued. "But they're reminding us that this isn't over. It's only when all three Thunder Eggs are returned that any of them will hatch."

"Any idea on what we should do with this one?" Zane spun the Thunder Egg on one finger like a basketball.

"They are saying not to show off with the

egg that contains a future ruler of Imperia," Yazmine said.

Zane laughed. "They are not saying that."

"Okay, they aren't saying that," Yazmine admitted. "But I am."

"What else?" Luca urged.

"That Dartsmith is angrier than ever. Apparently, he came here, to the Dragon Cave. He wanted information about us."

That confirms who left the human smell! Luca realized.

"Did he get anything out of them?" Zane asked.

"Of course not," Yazmine said.

Zane pumped the air with his fist. "Way to go, dead ancient dragons!"

Yazmine shushed him and tilted her golden head, listening to words only she could hear. "When the Ancient Ones refused to help him, Dartsmith sent the Avalanche Wolf in search of us. He knew we'd return. Wherever the wolf goes, it brings ice and snow with it. It is causing havoc throughout Imperia. The only way to stop Dartsmith is to get this egg to its nest."

"What nest?" asked Luca.

"We must cross the Frozen Sea and find the Ice Hotel," Yazmine reported, puffing smoke into the air. "The nest is in there. But we must be careful. The Ancient Ones keep saying this: The Avalanche Wolf is getting hungrier with each passing moment. Dartsmith has trained it to only eat when he allows it to do so. But if the wolf has to go much longer without food, who knows what it will do?"

Luca thought of the famished stare of those wolfish eyes. He studied the drawings on the cave's wall. The wave shapes must represent the Frozen Sea! And the palace-like thing must be the Ice Hotel.

Zane yelped. "That wave icon is flashing on the egg," he said. "Maybe that's the Frozen Sea? Ask the dragons, Yaz."

But once again, the cave was silent, dark, and gloomy.

Luca, Yazmine, and Zane hurried from the cave.

"Frozen Sea, here we come!" Zane said cheerily. "Luca, we can use the egg's map to find our way there. Yaz, you can follow me and Luca from above."

Luca stared at Zane. "Aren't you flying with Yazmine?"

"No, I'm going to run there. I'm superfast, after all." Zane grinned as he headed for the edge of the platform. "I'll race you!"

Luca sighed. The Frozen Sea was a long way away. And he really did not want to race Zane. But Zane had the map, and he couldn't risk losing sight of him.

"Good luck, you two," called Yazmine, rising elegantly into the air. "I have a feeling you're going to need it."

Zane and Luca headed down the mountain path. There was no doubt Zane was speedy. Superhumanly speedy! But he also wasted a lot of time. Once they were down the mountain and into the forest, Zane kept zipping off in different directions. He would disappear for a few minutes, then suddenly leap out from behind a boulder or a tree to try to scare Luca.

It never worked, though. Luca had amazing hearing as a beast. Besides, the forest birds kept Luca informed as to where Zane was at all times. Luca just concentrated on running at a steady pace. Sure, he wasn't as fast as Zane, but he felt like he could keep running forever.

In time, the forest began to thin out. The temperature dropped, and snow grew thicker. The sun was setting now, and the light made the snow shimmer.

Zane ran up from the opposite direction, his face alive with excitement. "Just wait until you see what's up ahead!"

The track curved around to the left. Luca stopped short, amazed. Off in the distance, a massive wave curved up into the darkening sky. Luca held his breath, waiting for it to crash. But the wave didn't move.

Luca squinted at the horizon. "The Frozen Sea!" He'd never seen anything so strange and magical. As he ran forward, more arches of bluish ice rose up, all looking as if they were about to fold back into themselves at any moment. But instead, they remained perfectly still. It was like time had stopped.

"We're getting close now," called a powerful voice from above. Luca scanned the sky, looking for Yazmine. Sure enough, there she was, swooping and twirling above them, catching the last of the daylight on her golden wings.

"Frozen waves would be *epic* to skate on." Zane grinned. "I wish I had my board with me. Maybe I can find a piece of wood to use instead?"

"Don't go running off again," Luca said. "We need to find the Ice Hotel, remember? It must be near here. We'd better locate it before it's too dark."

Zane looked at him with a funny expression.

"What?"

"Your fur is glowing," Zane said.

Sure enough, Luca's white fur had taken on a bluish-green color as the daylight disappeared.

"You know what?" Zane said thoughtfully. "With that fur, you'd be really useful on my football team when we play night games. Want me to teach you some skills?"

"No, thanks."

"C'mon! Why not?"

Luca gritted his teeth. Did he really have to remind Zane that back in the regular world, Luca didn't have fur at all? Let alone glow-in-the-dark fur?

"Football isn't really my thing," Luca said, hoping to drop the subject.

"Let's see about that," said Zane, and he shot ahead. When he was just a speck in the distance, he turned and yelled something. The words floated back to Luca. "Here, catch!"

To Luca's dismay, Zane threw the egg high into the sky. It spun through the air, lit up by sunset rays.

"What are you DOING?" Luca yelled. He sprinted toward the tumbling Thunder Egg. If the rock landed on this icy ground, it would surely smash. And who knew what would happen to Imperia then? Nothing good, that's for sure. Luca slid on his feet to position himself under the tumbling egg.

As he reached out his paws to catch the

precious egg, Luca heard a familiar whirring sound.

Oh no . . . He knew that sound only too well.

A mass of dark shapes swarmed closer. Dartsmith's surveillance bugs! Their bulging eyes clicked. Their mechanical wings buzzed.

Luca was determined to get to that egg before they did. He leapt into the air, stretching out his hairy paws. But the swarm of insect drones surrounded the egg, screeching with excitement.

Zane zipped back to help, but even together they were no match for the cloud of drones. The insects closed in tightly around the Thunder Egg.

Their spindly legs clicked together to form

a kind of huge flying cage. Then, with the Thunder Egg trapped inside, Dartsmith's drones rose into the air.

A shadow fell across the icy ground. A massive, dragon-shaped one.

"Don't even think about it!" Yazmine roared at the drones. Flames shot from her mouth, exploding into the cold evening air.

The golden dragon darted toward the cluster of drones, her powerful claws outstretched. The drones zipped from side to side, but there was no outflying Yazmine. She quickly caught up to them, and plunged her sharp talons into the mass of insect drones.

Hovering in midair, Yazmine gave the insect drones an almighty shake. The group split apart, drones scattering every which way.

"Go, Yaz!" urged Luca as he spotted the Thunder Egg. It was free from the drones, but now it was falling!

Yazmine tried to catch it, but drones flew at her face. She whirled around, lashing out at

them with her tail, and called to her teammates. "One of you, catch it!"

Zane leapt upward. But for once, Luca was
quicker. He wrapped his paws around the egg
and landed back on the ice with a thump. The
egg was safe once more!

Yazmine flew down and landed next to Luca and Zane. Zane hung his head low.

"I let our team down," Zane said mournfully, pointing at the egg in Luca's paws. It had a new score on it.

2:2

"I can't believe I nearly handed the Thunder Egg right to Dartsmith's buzzy drone pests."

Zane shook his head. "I'll make up for it, I promise."

Zane seemed truly sorry. A little reluctantly, Luca handed the egg back to him.

Yazmine stretched her wings. "Let's keep going."

Zane looked at her suspiciously. "Wait a minute. Aren't you going to get mad at me?"

"Oh, you totally messed up," Yazmine said, a plume of smoke curling from her nostrils. "But you know that already. And right now, we have to move on. Look!"

Up ahead was a magnificent building made entirely of ice. Surrounded by swirling snow, the building sparkled like crystal in the setting sun.

Luca knew at once what it was. "The Ice Hotel!"

The hotel's roof was dotted with twisting turrets. The beautiful windows each had ornate balconies. A row of enormous animal sculptures, all chiseled from ice, formed a pathway to the grand front entrance.

It was the fanciest hotel Luca had ever seen. Also, the coldest.

"Look at the map." Zane turned the egg around so the others could see the lines etched on it. The purple, gold, and white lights that represented Zane, Yazmine, and Luca were clustered near the Ice Hotel icon, which flashed wildly. "This is the place for sure."

He put the Thunder Egg back in his bag. A second later he was standing in front of the hotel's entrance. "Are you two coming or what?" he called cheerfully.

Yazmine rolled her eyes. "Doesn't take him long to bounce back, does it?" she muttered to Luca. "Come on, we'd better keep an eye on him. Who knows what damage Zane could do in a place made of ice."

Together, the teammates walked through the grand, icy-blue entrance of the hotel. They found themselves in an opulent foyer. The floor and walls were as smooth and shiny as a polished mirror. High up above them was a domed ceiling.

The cavernous space could fit hundreds of

people. But it was completely empty, except for a magnificent sculpture at its center. An enormous block of ice had been carved to look like a dragon sitting on a nest.

"I feel like that ice dragon is watching me," said Zane, raking his fingers through his hair nervously. "And check out that nest! It's big enough to take a bath in."

"That must be where we put the Thunder Egg!" Yazmine exclaimed.

Just then, a figure walked into the lobby from the side door. It was an elderly man with white hair and a back so hunched it was impossible to see his face. He was dressed in a silver fur coat and held a shining tray.

"You are correct," said the man, gliding

across the smooth floor with surprising speed. His feet barely seemed to touch the ground at all.

Luca's suspicion immediately took hold. There was something about this guy's bright blue eyes that Luca just didn't trust. His beast nose twitched. There was a bad smell in the air that even the tasty food could not mask.

"We've been expecting you at the Ice Hotel," the waiter said. "In fact, we've organized a little welcoming party for you. It is such an honor to have you here."

"A party? But where are the other guests?" Yazmine asked, looking around the huge empty space.

The waiter smiled thinly. "They are on their way. In the meanwhile, please help yourselves." He held out his tray.

"No, thanks," said Luca. The snacks looked amazing and hunger gnawed at his belly. But his beast instinct was telling him not to take anything offered by this person. Yazmine also shook her head.

Zane, on the other hand, grabbed as many of the snacks as he could, shoving them in his pockets.

"Zane!" hissed Luca. You didn't need to know anything about fancy hotels to know that stuffing your pockets with food was kind of rude.

But the waiter did not seem to care. In fact, his smile grew broader. "Why don't you empty your bag?" he suggested. "Then you could fill it with snacks as well. I will take care of anything that might be in it."

Luca's fur prickled. He felt a low, menacing growl rise in his throat. "Don't do it, Zane."

The waiter shot Luca a look. His blue eyes flashed with anger. Luca knew those eyes! He knew that sharp nose, too. And the strange smell? And he suddenly remembered where he'd encountered it before. It was in the Dragon Cave.

"Dartsmith!"

Instantly, the old man straightened up. He wasn't old at all. He tipped up the tray,

dumping the remaining food on the floor, then spun it at Zane's head. The tray's razor-sharp edge gleamed as it whirled.

"Watch out!" Luca and Yazmine yelled.

In a flash, Zane leapt to one side and the tray lodged into an icy wall like a dagger.

"Give me the egg!" Dartsmith yelled. He flung off his silvery coat and a cape billowed out like a storm cloud. Drones appeared, lifting and folding the edges of the cape into intricate shapes. In seconds it clicked into a new, jet-wings shape. "I will not have Imperia taken from me by children, beasts, and dragons! Give it to me now or you will pay the price!"

Yazmine rose into the air. "There's no way we're doing that!" she roared back. Golden flames leapt from her mouth and a section of ice wall immediately melted. "Not now. Not tomorrow. NOT EVER!"

"You will regret this!" Dartsmith snarled. He pulled out a whistle from under his cape and blew it. A strange, high-pitched noise filled the room. It was the same sound Luca had heard before the Avalanche Wolf had attacked!

Luca looked at the others. "Can you hear that?"

"Only lowly beasts can hear my whistle," Dartsmith sneered. "I believe you have already met the one I am summoning now."

Fear gripped Luca. Another sound had arisen. It was a deep booming, growing louder by the second. Soon angry howls joined the mix, bouncing off the walls of the Ice Hotel.

"I can definitely hear that," Zane said, his face pale.

"The wolf is coming," Yazmine said grimly.

Dartsmith clapped his hands in delight. "I

told you the other guests would be here soon! Beasts are very stupid but they are easy to train. I can't wait for you to see it perform its other tricks."

Drones flew beneath Dartsmith's jet cape, lifting him into the air.

Luca's paws were clammy and his pulse beat like a drum. He looked around the huge room, his mind spinning. More of Dartsmith's drones were swarming around the ice sculpture. It was going to be hard to get the Thunder Egg into its nest.

"Whatever is about to happen," Yazmine said, "we face it together, okay?"

"Darn right we do," Zane said. "But, um, do we have a game plan?"

Luca took a deep breath. "Our plan is to get the Thunder Egg into that nest. Yaz, you're the dragon so you'll have to do it. Remember what the Ancient Ones told us last time? *It takes a dragon to make a dragon.* Meanwhile, Zane and I will do whatever we can to keep Dartsmith distracted."

Yazmine nodded and whooshed into the air.

"Zane, it's time you put that hyperspeed of yours to the test. Do you think you can outrun a swarm of evil drones?"

Zane grinned. "Only one way to find out." There was a blur of color and suddenly Zane was on the other side of the huge room.

A moment later, a loud thud sounded and the entire hotel shuddered. Luca tensed, smelling danger in the air. What was going on? He could hear the bloodcurdling cries of the Avalanche Wolf outside. One of the hotel's ice walls began to crack.

Luca suddenly realized what was happening. The Avalanche Wolf was trying to bash down the frozen hotel walls!

By the looks of it, it was going to succeed very soon.

9

A crack zigzagged along the thick walls of the hotel, like a frozen lightning strike. Then, with a sound like shattering glass, one entire wall fell in, revealing the sky and a huge bank of snow.

The snowbank began to heave and lift, as if something was pushing its way out. From the snow leapt the Avalanche Wolf, bigger than ever. And with even more heads than last time!

The beast shook itself, sending snow flying.

"Bring me the egg!" Dartsmith screamed at the wolf, hovering above them.

"We must find the Thunder Egg," Luca heard one of the wolf heads growl. "Then Master will feed us."

Another head sniffed the air. "The human boy has it," snarled another as the creature crouched low, preparing to attack.

Luca's heart thumped in his chest. "Zane," he called. "Throw the egg to Yaz RIGHT NOW!"

Zane nodded and whipped the egg from the bag. "Yaz! Catch!" he yelled, tossing the egg in the dragon's direction.

Yazmine zoomed toward it. But before she could grab it, a cloud of Dartsmith's drones ambushed her, attacking her golden wings with their needlelike spikes. Yazmine roared, flames leaping from her mouth. Burned drones clattered to the ground. Yazmine darted forward again, reaching for the Thunder Egg. But just as her talons curled around it, more drones flew at her.

"Watch out, Yaz!" Luca warned.

But it was too late. Yazmine slammed into the icy wall of the hotel. The egg flew from her grasp, hurtling once more into the air. It flew up high, toward the domed roof of the hotel.

"My wing!" groaned Yazmine as she slid down the icy wall. "I—I can't fly."

"Ha! Lucky that I can!" Dartsmith called, flying toward the egg.

"Don't worry, guys. I've got this," called Zane.

But before he could move, the Avalanche Wolf leapt on him, covering him in a mountain of ice and snow.

"Zane!" Luca yelled.

"I'm okay," came a muffled voice from under all that snow. "Just grab the egg!"

At the beginning of this adventure, Luca had felt like a human pretending to be a beast. After his fight with the Avalanche Wolf, he'd felt like a failed beast. But right now, he felt his beasty side take over. He dropped to all fours and bounded toward the Thunder Egg.

He could see Dartsmith reaching his bony fingers out for the prize. Fury burned in him.

"Not going to happen!" growled Luca. Using every muscle he had, Luca leapt into the air, snatching the egg from Dartsmith's grasp. Luca tumbled to the ground, rolling carefully to protect the egg.

But there was no time to feel proud. With a roar, the Avalanche Wolf charged at Luca, snow streaming from its immense body.

Luca leapt to his feet, the egg tucked under one arm. A low snarl emerged from deep in his throat. His fear was totally gone, now replaced with frustration. "Why are you working for Dartsmith? He is no friend to us beasts. My pack and I are here to protect Imperia. Help us fulfill the prophecy together."

The wolf seemed to slow, just a little. Were Luca's words having an effect?

"Do not listen to the Outsider!" shrieked Dartsmith. "Whatever he is saying, it is false!"

The shrill sound of his whistle once again filled the room. Its high pitch bounced off the walls and shards of broken ice. For Luca it was like a hundred nails scraping on a blackboard.

The animal howled, its heads thrashing wildly. With so many ears, surely the whistle hurt this beast even more than Luca?

Soon the room grew white with blizzarding snow.

"Yaz!" Luca yelled. He couldn't see the golden dragon through the snow, but he hoped she could hear him. "Can you get close to the nest? When I get the chance, I'll throw you the egg."

"I'm on it," Yaz called through the haze.

"Zane?" Luca said. "Speak to me, bud! Where are you? Are you okay?"

There was no reply. Luca was about to call again when he heard a growl. Pivoting, Luca found himself staring into way too many pairs of pale-blue eyes. With a chorus of bloodthirsty snarls, the wolf leapt at him, its many jaws wide. But Luca's beasty reflexes were ready. He sprang up, landing on the monster's back.

Howling with rage, the many heads whipped around, spraying out blasts of snow. It fell all over Luca, making it hard to see and filling his throat and nose. *Was it possible to drown in snow?*

Luca dug his claws into the wolf's cold back, its icy fur crackling like pine needles. The wolf lifted its heads and snapped. Through the whirl of white, Luca glimpsed too many teeth, shining like blades.

Up above, Luca heard the buzz of Dartsmith's drones. "So you're hungry, are you?" Dartsmith asked the wolf heads. "Deliver the egg to me. Then you will eat!"

"He is not a good master!" Luca growled, holding on to the wolf's back with one paw and the egg with the other. "He doesn't look after you or Imperia. He only cares for himself!"

"You lie, beast! Dartsmith cares for us!" barked the Avalanche Wolf.

Riding an angry, multi-headed wolf with one hand was like the wildest rodeo ever. Luca was starting to get tired. How long could he keep this up?

It was then that Luca smelled something nearby. It smelled like . . . snacks?

A figure stepped out from a deep pile of snow. "Dinnertime!" Zane called in a cheery voice.

The wolf heads all turned on Zane, frozen in a moment of surprise. Zane began to pull food from his pockets, tossing treats at the open mouths of the wolf. The mouths gobbled them up greedily.

"Is that better?" Zane asked. He reached out and gently patted one of the heads.

"Um, Zane, I really don't—"

But before Luca could finish, the wolf sat on its hind legs. Luca slid off its back as the wolf leapt at Zane. Not to attack him, but to nuzzle him. It was quite a sight.

A shadow fell over them from above. "Stop

this at once! Attack the beast. We need that egg!" demanded a furious Dartsmith.

But the wolf ignored him. Right now it only had (lots of) eyes for Zane.

Zane stroked the many heads and grinned at Luca. "I have dogs at home. Kindness always works better than being a beast. No offense, Luca."

"None taken." Luca smiled.

"You WILL obey me!" screamed the red-faced Dartsmith, reaching for his whistle. He put it to his mouth and took a deep breath. But before he could blow on it, a snowball flew through the air, knocking the whistle out of his hands.

"Nice shot!" Luca called, leaping up and

grabbing the whistle as it fell. He crushed it between his paws as the golden dragon landed next to him.

"Thanks, Luca!" Yazmine said. "Pass me the egg? I think it's time to put it where it belongs, in the ice sculpture."

"Is your wing okay?" Luca asked as he passed Yazmine the egg.

"It's a bit sore," she admitted, wrapping her powerful talons around the precious rock. "But not sore enough to stop me doing this!" She flew across the room toward the sculpture.

With a shriek, Dartsmith swooped after her. Yaz turned and roared with all her might.

Golden flames surged from her mouth, blasting Dartsmith away. The smell of burning metal filled the air and singed drones began falling.

Without his drone army to keep him aloft, Dartsmith crashed to the icy floor.

"Wolf, destroy that sculpture," Dartsmith yelled weakly.

"How about we destroy YOU instead?" one of the heads snarled. "We were never hungry when the dragons were in charge."

Dartsmith paled, holding up his hands as the wolf padded toward him. "I am your master! You must not—"

His words were drowned by the snarls of

the wolf as it leapt at Dartsmith. There was a whirl of snow and the beast tumbled away through the broken walls of the Ice Hotel, taking Dartsmith with it.

"Hey! We just got another point!" Yazmine called from over near the sculpture. "Does that mean we've won this round?"

3:2

"Sure does!" yelled Zane, doing a few extra zips around the room to celebrate.

"Are we ready to do this?" Yazmine was still hovering next to the sculpture.

"Soooooo ready!" Luca and Zane called.

Yazmine pressed the Thunder Egg into the ice nest below the dragon. There was a satisfying click as the egg fit perfectly into place.

The incredible ice dragon glowed pink, then blue, then purple. The light intensified and a hypnotic hum filled the icy space. Words flashed up on the Thunder Egg.

Round two is complete. See you again for round three!

There was a burst of light as the remaining walls of the hotel shattered. All that was left standing in the frozen landscape was the enormous glowing dragon sculpture, protecting its egg.

Darkness enveloped Luca as the ground dropped away.

10

The smell of sweat and dirt flooded Luca's nostrils. Without opening his eyes, he knew he was back in the sports equipment room. Luca sat up and looked around. There was Yazmine, in human form again and already on her feet, checking her watch. Zane had somehow ended up in the cage where the balls were kept.

He climbed out, grinning at the others.

"That was even more fun than last time!"

Luca laughed. "Well, if by fun you mean terrifying, difficult, and dangerous, then yeah. I guess it was." He turned to Yazmine. "How long have we been gone?"

"Same as last time," Yazmine said. "Just a couple minutes."

A shrill sound filled the air. For a horrible moment, Luca thought it was Dartsmith's whistle. Then he chuckled. "The lunch bell."

"Lunch? What are we waiting for?" said Zane. "Luca, open the door for me and stand back. I want to test if any of that Imperia hyperspeed has stuck with me."

Luca held open the door for Zane, who

sprinted out . . . and almost knocked over Ms. Long!

"Oops, sorry, Ms. Long," said Zane, screeching to a stop. "I didn't see you there."

"Clearly," said Ms. Long dryly. "I was coming to check on whether you had succeeded."

Luca stared at their teacher. Did she mean had they succeeded in returning the Thunder Egg to Imperia?

Ms. Long strode over to the storeroom and inspected it. "Very good," she said approvingly. "I know that was a difficult task. But I was confident you three could do it. You worked together and did what was needed."

"Um, thanks," said Yazmine. Luca could tell

from her expression that she was as unsure as he was about what Ms. Long meant.

As their teacher began to walk away, Luca risked calling out a question. "Ms. Long? Do you think you'll need us to clean up anything else?"

Ms. Long turned and fixed him with serious eyes. "There is another very important job ahead of you," she said. "Probably the most challenging one yet. Much more difficult than cleaning up this storeroom."

Again Ms. Long's expression was impossible to read.

"And when will that be?" asked Zane.

"That is unknown," replied Ms. Long simply. "But right now, you three should go and have your break. Zane, you look like you need to run around a little. And Yazmine, I know you've been flying around all morning, but you should put on a sweater before you go outside. It's a little cooler today." Finally, she turned to Luca and brushed a hair off his shoulder. "Good grooming is very important, Luca," she said in a disapproving tone. "You're not some kind of a beast, you know."

"Sorry," muttered Luca.

As Ms. Long walked away, he thought he heard a little snort. Was it laughter? Luca couldn't be sure.

Once Ms. Long was gone, Luca turned to Yazmine and Zane. "See you guys next time, I guess."

It felt weird to just walk away after all they had been through together. But what else was there to do?

To Luca's surprise, Zane suddenly stuck out his hand. "You know what we need? A team handshake. We should celebrate."

Luca shot a glance at Yazmine. Team handshakes did not seem like the sort of thing she'd be into.

But Yazmine nodded. "Great idea." She put her hand over Zane's.

With a shrug, Luca added his to the top of the pile.

"Right, now we need a chant. Ooh! I've got one," Zane began to chant. "We're Team Dragon, Human, Beast. We're the best, to say the least!"

"Zane, that's terrible!" groaned Yazmine.

Luca laughed. The chant shouldn't work. But somehow it did. Which made it perfect for the three of them. And whatever the third round of the game turned out to be, Luca just knew they'd get through it the same way they'd gotten through the last two. Together.

DRAGON GAMES

Keep reading for a special sneak peek of

Dragon Games #3: *The Battle for Imperia*!

Luca hurried into the school cafeteria. Lunchtime was nearly over, but he had to eat something! As he was grabbing a tray, the doors swung open. A girl with dark hair and green eyes rushed in.

"Yazmine!" Luca was surprised. Yazmine was not the type of person who ran late for anything.

"I've been trying to make it here all lunchtime," Yazmine said, a little breathless as she also took a tray. "Ms. Long asked me to return some books to the library."

"She got me to take our camp forms to the principal. I just got here, too," Luca said.

He felt a little awkward. He and Yazmine didn't really talk much at school. They had totally different friend groups. But they had been on a couple of big adventures together in a mysterious land called Imperia. They were part of a three-person team trying to bring dragons back to Imperia.

Luca had seen Yazmine in dragon form. She'd seen him in dragon and beast form. But they'd never eaten lunch together.

"What would you like?" asked a bored-looking woman behind the counter.

There wasn't much food left. Luca and Yazmine looked at the gloopy pumpkin soup and shrivelled fries.

"I guess I'll take the soup, please," Luca said.

"Fries for me, thanks," Yazmine said.

As the server began dishing out their food, the cafeteria doors opened again. Someone hurried in, running his fingers through his hair. It was Zane: football star and third member of the Imperia team.

"Any food left?" he asked. "I'm starving!"

The woman serving smiled at him. She didn't look bored anymore. "You're Zane, right?"

This woman was new at the school cafeteria. How did she already know Zane's name?

But Zane didn't seem surprised. He was used to everyone knowing who he was. "Yup," Zane said cheerily.

The server reached below the counter. When she straightened up, she was holding a steaming bowl of spaghetti and meatballs.

"For you," she said, handing the bowl to Zane.

"Wait, what?" Yazmine said, outraged. "How come he gets that and we get sorry leftovers?"

"Special order," the woman shrugged. "You'd better eat quickly. Bell's going to ring in ten minutes."

Luca, Yazmine and Zane sat at the nearest table. A strained silence fell. The three of them never sat together at school.

Yazmine speared a soggy fry with her fork and nibbled the end. Luca looked at his soup. Maybe it tasted better than it looked? He tried it. Nope. Worse. Definitely worse.

Only Zane was enjoying his food.

Luca frowned. Why had Zane gotten a special meal?

Luca looked up as Ms. Long, their teacher, stuck her head around the half opened door. "Ah, there you three are. I am glad you're eating. You're going a lot of need energy this afternoon."

"Why?" Yazmine asked eagerly.

Clearly, she was thinking the same thing as Luca: Were they returning to Imperia?

Ms. Long just smiled. "I'll see the three of you later."

Then the door closed again.

"This is SO good!" Zane said, shovelling in mouthfuls of spaghetti.

Yazmine eyed it enviously. "That's a huge serving. There's no way you'll eat all that. How about you share?"

"Of course I'll eat it all." Zane looked insulted. "But sure, you can share."

"Thanks!" said Yazmine and Luca at the same time.

Zane was annoying sometimes, but he could also be generous.

Luca stuck his spoon into the spaghetti and tried to twirl the strands around it. As he lifted it, the pasta slipped off. He really needed a fork. He tried again, this time digging the spoon in deeper. His utensil hit something.

"There's something hard in there," Luca said.

"What do you mean?" Zane stuck his fork deep into the mountain of pasta. There was a muffled clink as Zane's fork made contact with . . . something.

The three teammates looked at one another.

Luca's pulse sped up. Something was about to happen. He could feel it.

Yazmine attacked the pasta, sending meatballs flying. One of them flicked out of the bowl, pinging Zane on the nose.

"Hey, careful!" he said, wiping off the sauce and then licking his finger.

Yazmine paid him no attention. "Look!"

There, at the bottom of the huge bowl was a rock, draped with strands of spaghetti.

Luca leaned forward. "Is that a Thunder Egg?" he asked doubtfully.

The last two Thunder Eggs they'd returned to Imperia had been football-sized. This thing was no bigger than a baseball.

"Come on, Luca! What else would it be?" Yazmine teased. "A giant meatball?"

"Maybe!" Zane grinned. "Let me check." Zane reached into the bowl. The moment his fingers took hold of the strange lump, the room plunged into darkness.

Excitement and nerves gripped Luca as he somersaulted through the inky blackness.

This was their third trip into Imperia. Where would they land this time? Would it be someplace new? It was also their third time competing against the power-hungry Dartsmith. This round would be the most important and dangerous of all.

Only when the three dragons return will Imperia have peace again.

Luca, Yazmine, and Zane had already returned two Thunder Eggs to the land. Inside these eggs were the future dragon rulers of Imperia. And now they had the third one. If Luca and his teammates managed to safely return this Thunder Egg to its rightful home, the ancient prophecy would be fulfilled.

And if they failed? Well, Luca didn't want to even think about that!

Luca felt the ground beneath him. The darkness faded, and Luca blinked as he looked around. He was near a stone wall—sturdy, ancient, and very high. Was it part of a building?

Luca stood up, brushing off the dirt and grass. He was no longer wearing his normal track pants. Instead he was wearing strange leather pants and heavy boots. At his feet was the Thunder Egg. It still had a single strand of spaghetti on it. Quickly, Luca removed the pasta and stowed the egg safely in the bag he found slung across his shoulders.

He was glad to be in charge of looking after it. During the last trip, Zane had been in charge of the Thunder Egg, and he had not been nearly careful enough.

"So you're the human this time!" said a voice.

It sounded like Zane but way louder. Luca had already guessed that Zane would be a dragon this time, but somehow it was still a surprise to see the transformation. Zane was a massive dragon, for one thing. Far bigger than Luca or Yazmine had been. His scales were a shiny gray, almost metallic. This made him look like he was wearing armor.

ABOUT THE AUTHORS

Maddy Mara is the pen name of Australian creative duo Hilary Rogers and Meredith Badger. Hilary is a writer and former publisher; Meredith is a writer, and teaches English as a second language. Together they have written or created many bestselling series for kids. Their most recent series is The Dragon Girls, which has over 1.5 million copies in print, and is available in multiple countries and languages. They both currently live in Melbourne, Australia. Their website is maddymara.com.